Giraffe Gets A Long Neck

Christopher Mlalazi

Copyright © Christopher Mlalazi

ISBN 9780-7974-9413-8
EAN 9780797494138
Published by Plum'Tree Books in 2013

© Illustrations by Aubrey Bango
Typeset & designed by Kudzai Chikomo at Multimedia Box

Once upon a time, all giraffes could climb trees. Though they lived on the ground, they climbed the trees to eat the tender leaves at the top, which they favoured. At that time their necks were short like those of all other animals.

The world was beautiful then, with plenty of big, tall trees, pretty flowers, green grass and rivers that always flowed with fresh water.

Vusa, a young and happy giraffe, spent almost of his time leaping from tree branch to tree branch in the valley with his friend Thabani, the monkey.

But then the valley started getting warmer and warmer as the climate changed, and the trees started getting fewer as they died under the hot sun.

At the same time, it so happened that the giraffes had a baby boom and their population suddenly increased.

With so many giraffes, more leaves were eaten, so that the few trees remaining in the valley became almost all bare.

The monkeys were very worried by this, for the trees were their world, where they lived and played and fed. The monkeys did not eat leaves, but fewer trees meant less fruit, which they did eat.

One day Papa Monkey came up to Thabani.

'I am very worried Thabani, my child,' he said.

'What is it, Papa?' asked Thabani. They were sitting at the top of a plum tree, enjoying the fruit.

'It is your friend Vusa, the giraffe,' Papa Monkey said.

Just then they saw a herd of giraffe climbing trees in front of them and starting to devour their leaves. Soon the trees were bare of leaves, and the giraffes moved on to other trees. They were like a swarm of locusts attacking a field of grass.

'What about my friend Vusa, Papa?' asked Thabani.

'Yes, I know that Vusa is your good friend,' Papa Monkey said. Then he sighed and was silent.

'What is it, Papa?' asked a worried Thabani.

'Giraffes are eating all the leaves from the few trees still left in the valley,' Papa Monkey said. 'That is not good. Soon all the trees will be bare.'

A bee buzzed past them and settled on the sugar of an overripe plum that had burst open, and started feeding on it.

'That's right, Papa,' said Thabani. 'The trees need their leaves.'

'There is more,' continued Papa Monkey. 'Trees breathe in the carbon dioxide we breathe out and change it to oxygen, which they breathe out for us to breathe in. They use their leaves to do that.'

'But giraffes do not eat anything else, Papa,' said Thabani. 'If they do not eat the leaves they will starve.'

'But our valley also needs the leaves in order to survive, Thabani,' Papa Monkey said. 'You have to talk to Vusa about this if your friendship with him is to continue.'

'I will go and talk with him right now, Papa,' Thabani said. He straightaway leapt from the plum tree to the next tree, in the direction of the feeding giraffes.

Thabani found Vusa playing near the top of a tree as the rest of the giraffe family fed on the leaves nearby. He called him to come to the ground, and Vusa leapt down. The two friends sat on stones under the tree.

'Vusa, Papa says trees are getting fewer and fewer in the valley because of climate change,' Thabani explained.

'All the giraffes are worried about that too,' replied Vusa. 'If all the trees in the valley die from the hot sun we are going to starve as we can't eat anything else.'

'That is the point,' said Thabani. 'I told Papa that too, but he says the valley also needs the leaves from the few remaining trees to survive, and giraffes are eating them all up.'

'We too know about that,' said Vusa. 'We discussed that with all the giraffe families and we couldn't find any way out. Leaves are our food and we can't do without them.'

'And it's not just the fault of the giraffes, my dear friend, that trees are disappearing. If there was no global warming there would be enough trees to meet all the needs of the valley.'

'But what are we going to do?' asked Vusa. There were now tears in his eyes. 'You know I for one can try to change and eat grass, but the other giraffes say they will never stop eating leaves even if it leads to trees becoming extinct.'

Suddenly, a bee settled on the ground between the two animals. Thabani was sure it was the same bee he had seen on the plum tree earlier. The bee was now carrying a leaf that was a glowing green. Thabani and Vusa had never seen such a leaf in all their lives, and they stared at it in amazement.

'I have been listening to your conversation,' Bee said. 'I am humbled by your deep friendship despite your natural differences, and I think I might have a solution for you.'

'You do?' exclaimed Thabani.

'Is it a good one that will allow me and Thabani to remain good friends?' asked Vusa.

Bee looked at Vusa. 'Vusa, your giraffe family lives on the ground but climbs trees to feed on leaves,' he said.

'That is right,' replied Vusa. 'We giraffes prefer the tender leaves at the top of the tree.'

Bee looked at Thabani. 'Thabani, your family lives in the trees, but you do not feed on the precious leaves, but only on the fruit up there.'

'Yes, you are right,' said Thabani. 'Trees are our home.'

'Then the solution is simple,' said Bee. 'Giraffes have to remain on the ground where their home is, and the monkeys in the trees where their home is.'

'But how are we going to feed on the trees if we remain on the ground?' asked a worried Vusa.

'Trees are tall and we have to climb them to get to the leaves.'

'That is also simple,' said Bee. 'Just eat this leaf I have brought you and the answer shall be given.' He handed the glowing leaf to Vusa.

Vusa eyed the leaf suspiciously. 'If I eat the leaf it won't harm me?' he asked Bee.

'No it won't,' Bee assured him. 'Just be brave and eat it. I promise you your friendship with Thabani will become deeper. That is what both of you want, isn't it so?'

'Let me eat it for him,' Thabani offered.

'No, let Vusa eat it himself,' said Bee.

A tremulous Vusa took the leaf and he chewed it and swallowed. Suddenly, a change came over Vusa's body. First, his short legs grew longer, lifting his body up. And then his neck grew longer, until it reached the bottom leaves of the tree under which they were sitting.

Thabani looked around him. All the giraffes that were up in the trees began to float down to the ground. Like Vusa, their necks and legs had grown.

***

From that time on, giraffes could no longer climb trees to eat the tender leaves at the top, but their long legs and necks enabled them to reach up to eat the bottom leaves of the trees. In this way the leaves at the top of the trees were saved, providing the valley with precious oxygen, shade and beauty.

Vusa, the giraffe, could still talk and play with his friend Thabani, the monkey, while he stood on the ground and Thabani was in his home at the top of a tree.

Thabani and Vusa could sometimes be seen hiking across the once again flourishing valley, with Thabani hanging from Vusa's long neck, with a bee carrying a glowing leaf buzzing over them.